CAPTAIN DUCK

For Dad with love

First published in Great Britain by HarperCollins Publishers Ltd in 2002

1 3 5 7 9 10 8 6 4 2
ISBN: 0 00 713010 4

Jez Alborough

CAPTAIN DUCK

Collins

An imprint of HarperCollins Publishers

Pop, pop, coughs the spluttering truck.
'No more petrol left,' quacks Duck.

'It's good I stopped
near my friend Goat –

he uses petrol
in his boat.'

Duck rap-tap-taps at Goat's back door,
waits a while, then taps once more.

Still no answer, so instead,

he sneaks a peek inside Goat's shed.

'Hooray!' cries Duck. 'A stroke of luck –

petrol for my
thirsty truck.

I'll only take a drop or two…
Look, there's Frog! Where's he off to?'

He's off to take a trip on a boat.
'Hello!' calls Sheep. 'Hop in!' says Goat.

'There's one last thing I need to bring…
Now while I'm gone, don't pull that string.'

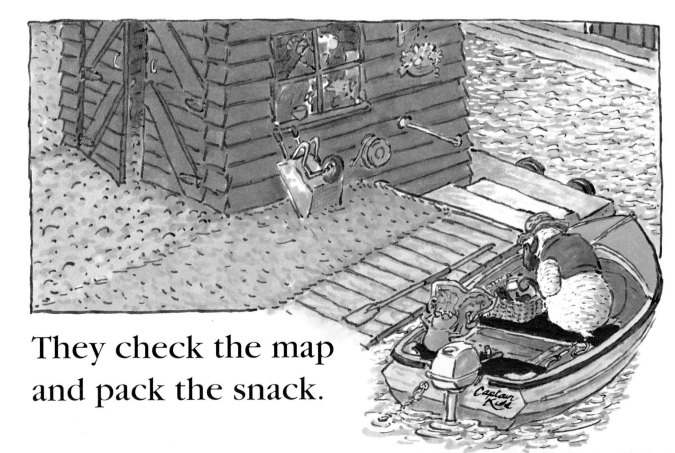

They check the map
and pack the snack.

Then suddenly,
they hear a quack.

'Ahoy there, sailors!' comes a cry.

'Is this a boating trip I spy?

If there are seas to be explored,

make way… CAPTAIN DUCK'S ON BOARD!

Let's get going!
What's this thing?'

'No!' cries Frog.
'Don't pull that string!'

The engine roars, Frog gives a shout.
'Oh, no!' screams Sheep. 'Frog's fallen out!'

PLOP

'Grab that rope,' says Duck. 'I'll steer.
Throw it out when we get near.

Ready…steady…get set…THROW!
Catch!' yells Duck. 'And here we go.

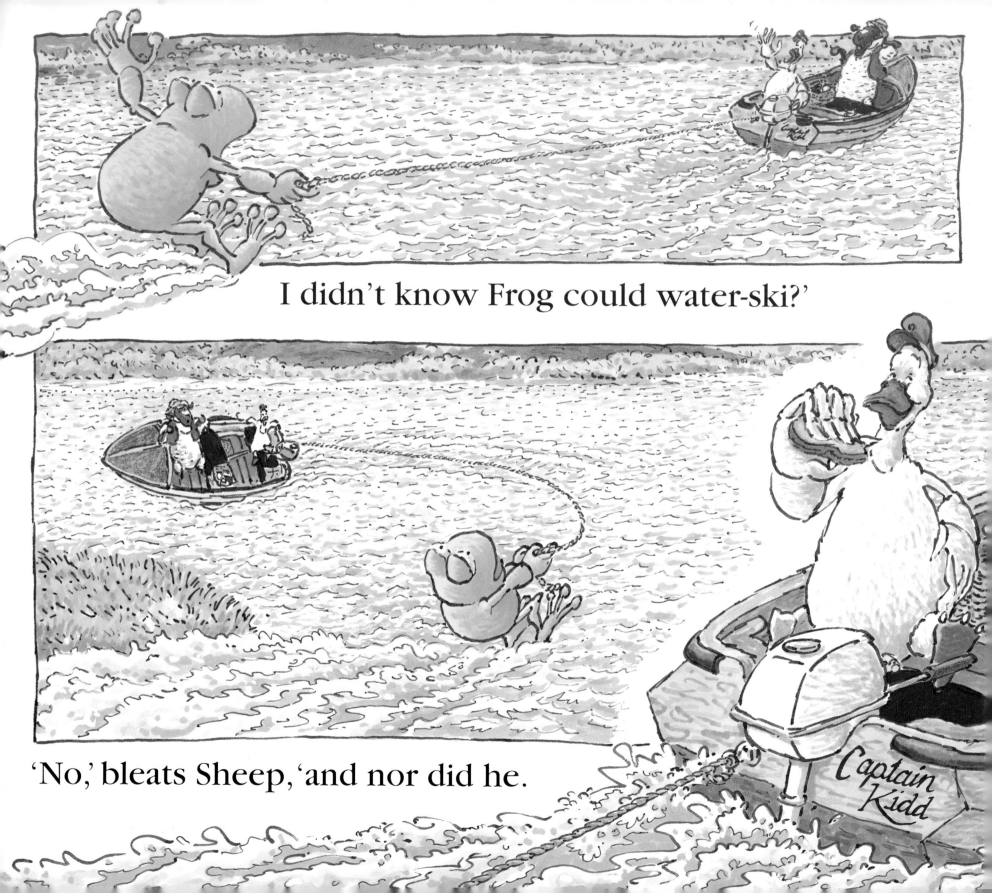

I didn't know Frog could water-ski?'

'No,' bleats Sheep, 'and nor did he.

Oh, please, Duck. Please don't go too far.

Goat will wonder where we are.
I think you'd better stop it now…'

'I can't,' yells Duck. 'I don't know how.   Besides we've only just begun…

and Frog is having so much fun.'

So Captain Duck steers the boat   far away from poor old Goat who finds his can beside a truck.

'Aha!' he says. 'That naughty Duck.'

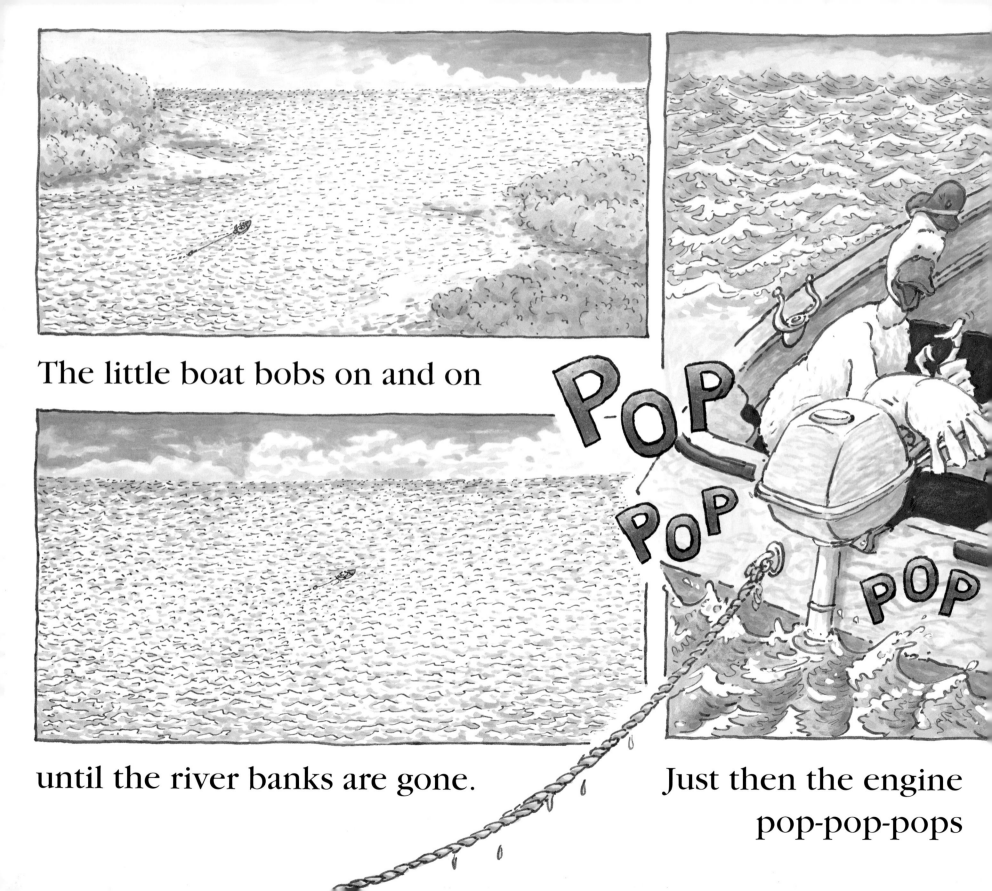

The little boat bobs on and on

until the river banks are gone.

Just then the engine
pop-pop-pops

and with a final cough
it stops.

The stormy waves begin to swell.
Sheep says, 'I don't feel too well.'

'Come on,' says Duck, 'we'll row to shore.'

'We can't,' gasps Frog.

'There's just one oar.'

They huddle in the bobbing boat
and snuggle close to Sheep's warm coat.

And there upon the restless deep

three lost friends fall fast asleep.

Through the night,
hour by hour,

Goat keeps lookout
from his tower.

And then at dawn,
   through bleary eyes,   upon the tide,   his boat he spies.

Sheep calls out, 'We're sorry, Goat.
We left you here...   we broke your boat!'

'Broken?' says Goat as Duck tries to hide.
'Oh, no, it just needed petrol inside.

That's why I went back for the can I keep spare.
I searched through my shed but the can wasn't there.'

'Wait!' says Frog. 'Duck was holding a can!
It was just before our boat trip began.

So Duck took the petrol.'   'That's right,' says Goat.
'Now you know why there wasn't enough in the boat.'

'Look! Duck's getting away!' Sheep cries.
'No, he's not!' gloats Goat with a glint in his eyes.

'He took the petrol,
that silly Duck,

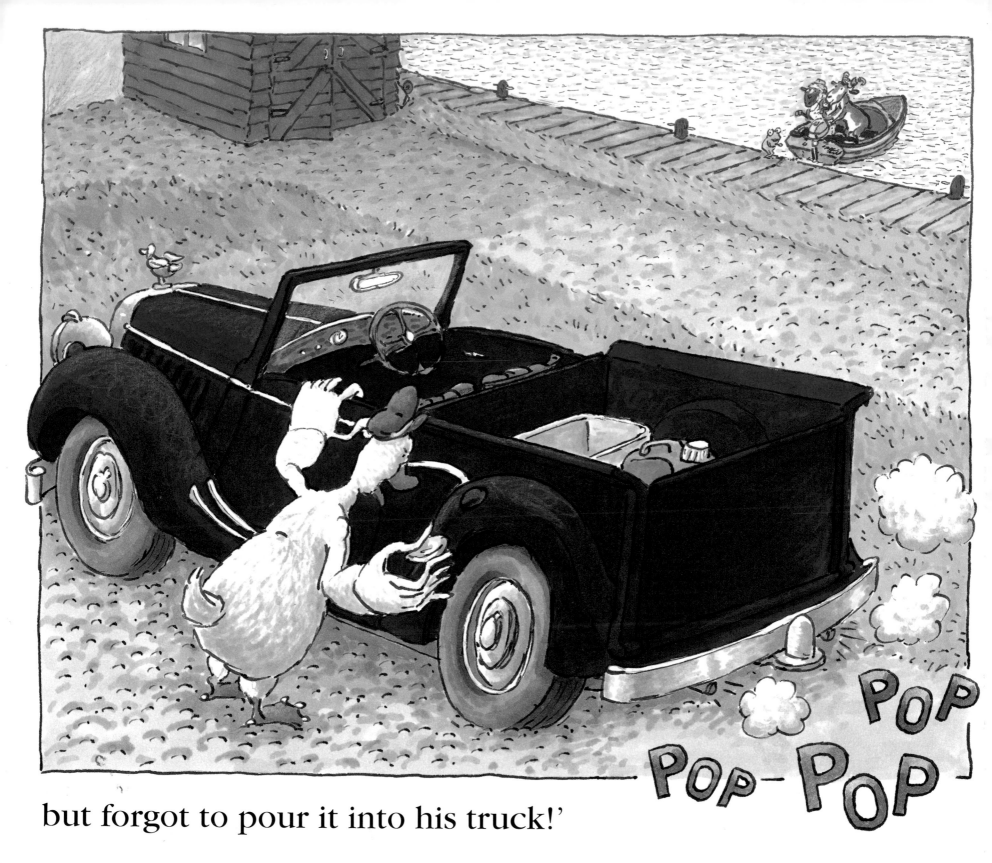

but forgot to pour it into his truck!'